Any references to historical events, real people, or real places are used fictitiously. Names, characters, and places are products of the author's imagination.

The Forest Detective Solving Mysteries in the Wilderness

By Ben Omar Ramdan

ISBN: 9798388395788

Ethan was hiking through the woods, his eyes darting back and forth as he took in the sights and sounds of the forest. As he walked, he noticed a strange object in the distance. Curious, he quickened his pace, eager to see what it was.

As he got closer, Ethan could make out the object more clearly. It was a small, shiny metal box, about the size of his hand. Ethan had never seen anything like it before, and he wondered what it could be.

Picking up the box, Ethan examined it closely. It was heavy and solid, with intricate designs etched into the metal. Ethan was fascinated by the box and wondered if it had any historical significance.

Determined to solve the mystery, Ethan decided to become a forest detective and set out to uncover the truth behind the box.

He started by examining the area around the box for clues. He noticed a set of footprints leading away from the box, and he followed them deeper into the forest.

As he followed the footprints, Ethan encountered various challenges and obstacles that tested his skills and knowledge of the wilderness.

Despite the challenges, Ethan persisted and continued to follow the footprints. As he got closer to the source, he realized that the footprints belonged to a family of hikers who had passed through the area earlier in the day.

Ethan was disappointed that he didn't find any more clues, but he was still determined to learn more about the box. He decided to bring the box home and do some research.

Back at home, Ethan spent hours researching the box's history, using books and the internet to gather information. He learned that the box was a rare artifact that had been lost for centuries, and that it was worth a lot of money.

Ethan was thrilled to have found such an important object and decided to work with his friends to ensure its safekeeping. He knew that the box was too valuable to be left lying around in the woods, and he was determined to protect it at all costs.

Excited by his discovery, Ethan realized that he had a newfound passion for exploration and solving mysteries in the wilderness. He knew that this was just the beginning of his adventures and that there were many more mysteries waiting to be uncovered.

Ethan searched for clues, day and night To solve the mystery, with all his might He questioned suspects, tall and small in search of answers, he would not stall

From the wise old owl, to the busy bee
Everyone had a theory, but which would it be?
Ethan listened closely, to what they had to say
Taking notes, and storing them away

He scoured the forest, from top to bottom
Looking for clues, like a detective's anthem
With a magnifying glass, he examined each lead
Trying to solve the mystery, with speed

Ethan's determination was strong, unwavering
To solve the mystery, and find out everything
With each new clue, his excitement grew
He knew he was getting closer, it was true

But still, the mystery remained unsolved
And Ethan knew, he had to be bold
To search for new leads, to solve the case
And to do it all, with a smile on his face.

Ethan searched high and low
For a new clue, to help him grow
He searched with his friends, with all their might
But the answer seemed to stay out of sight

That's when a chipmunk appeared
And Ethan's problem suddenly cleared
The chipmunk knew something, he had no doubt
Ethan listened intently, as he talked about

The chipmunk told him about a secret path
Hidden deep within the forest's bath
A path that only he knew
That could lead to the answer, and help him pursue

Ethan was grateful, for the chipmunk's help
And he knew that with it, he could find out the kelp
Together, they set out on the path
Hoping it would lead them to the aftermath

They walked and walked, for what seemed like miles
Through the thick trees, and the winding styles
Until they finally reached the end
And Ethan knew, he had a new friend

The path led to a hidden cave a place no one had ever
dared to brave but Ethan was brave, and he went inside
With the chipmunk by his side

Inside the cave, Ethan found a clue something that would
help him see it through and he knew that with the
chipmunk's help he was closer to solving the mystery,
with a yelp.

Ethan and his friends, with the chipmunk too
Decided to venture into the cave, and follow through
The darkness was deep, and the air was stale
But Ethan was determined, and he would not fail

With a flashlight in hand, they marched ahead
Through the twists and turns, and the narrow thread
They felt their way, through the rocky ground
And suddenly, a new clue was found

A glimmering light, from deep within
Ethan knew, that they were about to win
They pressed on, with renewed vigor
And soon enough, they found the trigger.

The light was coming from a gem so bright and a treasure so rare, it was quite a sight ethan knew, this was what he had been looking for and he could not wait, to explore it more

But suddenly, the ground began to shake
The walls started to tremble, and Ethan's heart did ache
He knew they had to get out, and fast before the cave
collapsed, and their journey wouldbe a thing of the past

With the gem in hand, Ethan and his crew ran as fast as
they could, to escape the cave's view and just in time,
they made it out but Ethan knew,
they had to do without

The mystery was solved, and the treasure was found
And Ethan knew, that with his friends around
Anything was possible, if they worked together
And that's what made their adventure, all the better.

Ethan and his friends, with the gem in tow were on
their way home, with spirits aglow
But something still nagged at Ethan's mind
A missing piece,
that he still had to find

He looked at the gem, and saw a small key hidden within
its depths, it was hard to see ethan knew,
this was what he had been seeking the final piece,
that would complete his seeking

He examined the key, and searched for a lock that it might
fit, like a jigsaw's clock he looked high and low,
And searched around but no lock was found,
to be newly crowned

That's when a wise old owl appeared and Ethan's problem,
suddenly cleared the owl knew something,
he had no doubt ethan listened intently,
as he talked about

A hidden chest, deep within the woods that could only be
opened, with the key's good, Ethan with the owl in sight
Set out on a new journey, with all their might

They searched and searched, for what seemed like days through
the thick brush, and the winding ways until they finally
reached the place where the chest lay,
in a hidden space

The key fit perfectly, and the chest popped open revealing
a treasure, that was quite a token
Ethan's heart swelled with joy, at what he saw
And he knew, he had discovered something raw

The mystery was solved, and the treasure was found
Ethan and his friends, had explored the woods and the ground
They had worked together, and overcome each trial
And Ethan knew, they had truly gone the extra mile.

Ethan and his friends, had completed their quest but now
it was time, to put their skills to the test for a storm
was brewing, and it was quite dire
Ethan and his friends, knew they had to inspire

The animals in the woods, were scared and afraid
They needed help, from the group that had made
The journey before, and knew the way
To safety and shelter, from the storm's fray

Ethan and his friends, worked together once more
To gather the animals, and lead them to a door
A barn nearby, where they could take cover
And ride out the storm, and not be a rover

They gathered the rabbits, and the squirrels too the deer
and the foxes, and all those who needed a helping hand,
to make it through the storm that was coming,
with all its might and hue

Ethan and his friends, led the way through the wind and
the rain, they did not stray until they reached the barn,
and opened the door and let the animals in,
to be safe once more

The storm raged on, but the group was unphased for they
had helped those, who needed it most in this craze
And Ethan knew, that this was what it was all about
Helping those in need, and not to doubt

The storm eventually passed, and the sun came out, Ethan
and his friends, had done their part, no doubt
And Ethan knew, that this was not the end
For he would continue to help, and be a true friend.

They saw a waterfall, that cascaded down
A sight so beautiful, they could hardly frown
They listened to the birds, that sang a sweet tune
And watched as the fireflies, lit up the night like a moon

Ethan and his friends, realized something new that the forest's
beauty, was a gift to view and they knew,
That it was up to them to preserve and protect,
this natural gem

They picked up trash, and cleared debris to ensure the forest,
remained clean and debris-free they helped the animals,
that were in need and planted new trees,
To replenish and feed

The forest was alive, with a beauty so rare and Ethan and
his friends, were eager to share their love for this place,
that had become so dear and they knew,
That it was up to them to steer

The future of the forest, for generations to come to
protect and preserve, this natural outcome
And Ethan knew, that this was his true call
To be a steward of nature, and protect it for all.

stumbled upon a mystery symbols etched on trees,
and rocks, in history they were curious,
and wanted to find out what these symbols meant,
without a doubt

They searched the woods, high and low for clues and answers,
that they could sow they studied the symbols,
and made a plan to solve the mystery,
and understand

They followed the trail, that the symbols made through
the woods, and the sun's shade until they reached
a clearing, in the glade and found a stone,
That was quite forbade

On the stone, were more symbols, they saw Ethan and
his friends, gasped in awe For they realized,
that this was the key to solving the mystery,
And setting it free

They deciphered the symbols, one by one and uncovered
a secret, that had been undone a treasure hidden,
in the woods for years that had been forgotten,
and shed no tears

Ethan and his friends, worked together to find the treasure,
and unearth the treasure and when they did,
they could hardly believe the treasure they found,
was beyond conceive

It was a chest, full of gold and jewels and Ethan and his
friends, felt like fools for they had thought,
it was just a tale but now they knew,
that it was for real

They divided the treasure, among them all and realized,
that this adventure, had a ball and Ethan knew,
that this was a story that would live on,
in all its glory.

Ethan and his friends, with a treasure found decided to
explore, beyond the usual ground they ventured into
the wild, so vast and free to discover new things,
that they couldn't foresee

They hiked through valleys, and up the hills and crossed the
streams, with little thrills they encountered creatures,
they'd never seen Like bears and moose,
that roamed so keen

They learned to build, a fire at night and cooked their food,
under the starry light they slept in tents,
that they set up fast and listened to the sounds,
of nature that cast

Ethan and his friends, felt so alive as they explored the wild,
with no jive they felt a sense of freedom,
they couldn't deny and embraced the wilderness,
with an open eye

They hiked for days, without a plan and saw the beauty,
of nature's grand stand they took in the sights,
and felt the breeze and watched the sunset,
with such ease

And when they returned, to their home base Ethan and his
friends, had a new trace of adventure, and discovery,
in their soul and a love for nature,
that they couldn't control

For they knew, that the wild, was a treasure to behold
And Ethan knew, that this adventure, was gold.

Ethan and his friends, were on a hike When they stumbled
upon, a dangerous sight a swarm of bees, buzzing around
Creating a threat, that was quite profound

They knew they had, to act fast to avoid the danger, that
was cast They remembered, what they had learned
And decided to act, with great concern

They covered their faces, and stayed calm and slowly, moved
away, with no alarm but the bees, were still in pursuit
And they knew, they couldn't just refute

Ethan and his friends, then found a tree and climbed up high,
as quick as can be they waited there, till the bees had gone
And knew, that they had, finally won

But as they climbed down, they heard a growl and saw a bear,
that made them scowl It was angry, and on the prowl
And they knew, they had to disavow

They stayed still, and kept quiet and watched the bear,
with a fright it sniffed around, and looked about
And then, finally, wandered out

Ethan and his friends, were relieved and knew, that they had,
achieved they had faced, a dangerous threat
And survived, with no regret

For they had learned, a valuable lesson to always stay, with
great caution and to never let, danger win
And to always come out,
with a grin

Ethan and his friends, were on their way to the forest, where
they could play but as they walked, they heard a sound
Of people chanting, all around

They followed the noise, and soon they saw a group of people,
standing tall they held up signs, that said "Save the Trees"
And shouted loud, with great unease

Ethan and his friends, then learned that a developer, had
planned to burn the forest down, to build a mall
And they knew, they had to answer the call

They joined the protest, with great might and chanted loud,
with all their sight they held up signs, that said "Save the
Woods"and knew, they had to do what they could

The developer, then came to see the protest, that had formed
a plea he listened to their words, and saw their stance
And finally, decided to give a chance

He changed his plans, and saved the trees and thanked the
protest, for helping him see that the woods, were important
and grand and that we should protect them,
in every land

Ethan and his friends, were proud of what they had, achieved
out loud for they had saved, a piece of land
And made a change, that would forever stand

They knew, that this adventure, had taught them to always
stand up, for what they thought and to never give up,
on what is right and to always fight,
with all their might·

Ethan and his friends, had a day of fun in the woods,
under the sun but as the day, drew to a close
They found themselves, in a tight pose

For they realized, that they were lost and the woods,
came with a great cost they tried to retrace,
their steps back but the path, was lost in the track

They walked and walked, for what seemed like miles but
they couldn't find, any familiar styles and as night fell,
they felt the fear af being lost, in the woods so near

They tried to make, a fire to keep warm and to stay awake,
and not get forlorn but as the night wore on,
they grew tired and their spirits, became more wired

But then, a chipmunk, came to their aid and showed them,
a path that they hadn't made they followed it,
with hope and trust and finally found,
a way out of the bust

They emerged, from the woods, to their surprise and saw
the sun, rise up in the skies they felt relief, and joy,
and glee and knew that they had,
finally been set free

Ethan and his friends, thanked the chipmunk for leading them,
out of the woods so bunk and they knew,
that this adventure, had taught them to never give up,
and to never be caught

For they had escaped, from the woods so great and Ethan
knew, that this adventure, was fate.

Ethan and his friends, entered the cave with their flashlights,
so they could pave their way through, the darkness ahead
And discover the secrets, that were unsaid

They saw stalactites, hanging down and stalagmites, that rose
from the groundthey walked through tunnels, and narrow path
And discovered a chamber, with a loud splash

There was a waterfall, that fell so high and a pool of water,
that caught their eye they wondered, what secrets,
it could hold and decided to explore, and be so bold

They swam through the pool, with great care and saw a
tunnel, that led somewhere they followed it,
with excitement in their hear and discovered, a room,
that was so art

The walls were covered, with drawings and art and they knew,
that it was so smart they realized, that it was ancient
And wondered, how long it had been dormant

They examined the drawings, with great awe and saw that it
told, a story so raw of a tribe, that lived in the past
And their culture, that had been cast

Ethan and his friends, then realized that this adventure,
was a great prize for they had discovered,
a piece of history that would always remain, a great mystery

They knew, that this cave, had so much to tell and that they
had uncovered, a secret so well and they promised,
to always remember this adventure, that they would forever
treasure·

Ethan and his friends, found a box that was hidden, behind some rocks they wondered, what it could hold
And decided to open it, so bold

They pulled off the lid, with great care and saw a book, that was so rare it was covered in dust, and so old
And they knew, that it was worth gold

They opened the book, with a gentle touch and saw that it was, a map so much it showed the forest, in great detail
And they knew, that it was not a fail

They followed the map, with great speed and found themselves, where they should lead they saw a tree, that was so tall and realized, that it was not small

They looked up, and saw a branch that was so high, and hard to catch but they knew, that it was the key
To discovering, the box's mystery

Ethan climbed the tree, with great skill and reached the branch, with a great thrill he saw a nest, that was so big
And knew, that it was not a fig

He reached inside, and felt around and found a key, that was so sound he climbed down, with a great speed and unlocked the box, with the key he freed

Inside the box, they found a note that said "This box, is not a joke it holds the purpose, of the forest's core and you have found it, now explore"

Ethan and his friends, then realized that this adventure, was not so disguised for they had found, the purpose of the woods and knew, that they had done so good

They promised, to always remember this adventure, that they would forever treasure and to always respect, the forest's core For they knew, that it was so much more·

Ethan and his friends stumbled upon a mysterious box and curiosity took over, they couldn't resist the locks they found an ancient map inside, with intricate detail leading to a tree, with a branch that would unveil

The key to the box, hidden in a bird's nest so high ethan climbed up with ease, not even a little shy he unlocked the box and found a note so profound the purpose of the forest, now they were all spellbound

They realized the importance of the nature around and vowed to respect it, forever to be found their adventure had taught them a valuable lesson to appreciate the beauty, and protect it with passion

Ethan and his friends, had a thirst for more they wanted a challenge, they wanted to explore and so they set off, to a distant land with their backpacks, and a map in hand

Their journey was long, and full of surprises they encountered new creatures, and exotic prizes the forest was different, with trees so tall and the air, had a fragrance, like a forest's call

They faced new challenges, that tested their might and pushed themselves, to the limits, so bright they learned new skills, and tried new things and discovered, a new world, with wings

Their adventure, took them far and wide and they felt a sense of joy inside for they had discovered, a new land so rare And explored it, with a curious stare

As they returned, to their home so dear they realized, that their journey, was clear for they had grown, in ways o true and found a love, for the world so new.

After successfully solving the mystery of the object, Ethan
becomes a respected forest detective in the community.
He continues to explore the forest and help protect its
wildlife and natural resources, while also sharing his
knowledge and love for the wilderness with others.

One day, while on a hike with his friends, Ethan comes
across a group of people who are illegally
logging trees in the forest. Using his detective
skills and quick thinking, Ethan is able to gather
evidence and bring the loggers to justice.

With his bravery and commitment to protecting the
forest, Ethan becomes a role model for others, inspiring
them
to follow in his footsteps and work to preserve
nature for future generations. The story ends
with Ethan looking out over the forest,
feeling proud of all that he has accomplished
and excited for the adventures that still lie ahead.

Made in United States
Troutdale, OR
02/19/2024

17819901R00029